MIRROR OF LIES

A JESSICA SMITH MYSTERY, SUSPENSE BOOK 1

AVA S. KING

I want to dedicate this book to my family and friends.
You are always with me, no matter where I go, and everything
you've taught me has made me a better person.

INTRODUCTION

Sign-up to Ava S. King's mailing list for news, new releases and special offers.

www.authoravasking.com

DISCLAIMER

This work of fiction contains strong language and explicit content and is only intended for mature readers. This story may contain unconventional situations, language, and sexual encounters that may offend some readers. This book is for mature readers (18+).

SYNOPSIS

Alison and Jessica were the best of friends in middle and high school. Fifteen years later, Jessica, now an up-and-coming journalist, learns that Alison has been killed in a car accident. But that's not the most troubling part of this tragedy.

Alison died with a secret that only she, Jessica, and a small group of friends knew. Her fear is that the secret didn't die with her friend.

If it didn't, what does that mean for her and the others who know what happened all those years ago?

LATEST RELEASES:AVA S. KING

PROLOGUE

The sun was setting around six-thirty in the afternoon, as it normally did every day during the summer for the past few months in Memphis. Jessica wasn't trying to stay cooped up in her folks' house while other children her age played in the street and partied until eight or nine at night. In her mind, they were lucky not to have strict parents or grandparents who would hound you about every little thing.

She had just turned thirteen and felt like an adult, even though her two best friends had recently gotten their periods. Jessica wanted to appear grown and important like her friends, so she applied lipstick and removed her hair from the everyday ponytail she usually kept it in. She was pulling her white shirt up, tying it into a knot to show off her stomach. Things that only happened when she was away from her grandparents' home, and when it was time to go back, she'd change back into her regular glasses, ponytail, and no makeup.

She snuck off to the barn where most kids her age and older would hang out and drink beer. Sometimes she'd see couples making out, and she often dreamed what it would feel like to kiss a boy. Jessica followed behind her friends Alison, Marnie, and

Lainey. Alison was the oldest at fourteen, the most strong-willed and outgoing. Marnie was the youngest at twelve, and Lainey was thirteen. During the summer three years ago, the group of four met when Jessica's parents had sent her to stay with her grandparents in their small town after they diagnosed her mother with cancer. After she went into remission, Jessica wanted to continue hanging with her friends, and she loved being spoiled by her grandparents.

While walking, Jessica put her hand up to block out the last of the sun as it drew down, and she grinned, seeing the barn wasn't too far out, and there wasn't a crowd of people hanging around. She waved toward Lainey to hurry because she couldn't be out too much longer or she'd get grounded. In her estimation, she had about an hour of fun left before she had to be back in the house. Dorothea and Marvin Lansbury didn't play about curfew or disobeying rules; often, her mother, Shirley, would quote them to stay in a child's place. Jessica giggled, picking up her pace, jogging toward her destination.

"Here, take this." Alison passed Jessica her bookbag and pushed open the shed door. The place sat near a lake and was over twenty years old. Lainey started climbing the ladder on the side and Marnie followed behind her as Alison wiped the sweat off her face. Alison reached into the bookbag that Jessica held, taking out a flashlight.

"Do you smell that?" Marnie muttered, holding a hand over her nose, kicking the trash bags out of her way as she strolled inside. An unusual odor wafted in the air over the large, rather ruinous and unstable dilapidated building. Dirt, opened food containers, and bottles of alcohol lay on the ground.

"Probably a dog or something," Alison replied, reaching in her bookbag and grabbing a bottle of beer. Marnie shrugged her shoulders, taking the bottle out of Alison's hand and following out to the edge of the barn doors near the lake. Lainey pulled herself up, wiping the dirt off herself and looking around the room. She didn't enjoy coming to the barn, but she wanted to fit in with her friends and not be labeled the nerd. Lainey was short, with shoulder-length brown hair, an oval-shaped face, small pointy nose, and a small, athletic build. She possessed a quiet nature that some people took to mean she was a pushover.

"Aghhhhh!" She heard a scream from Jessica and ran toward the sound, not looking where she was going, and tripped, falling on her face.

"Dummy," she mumbled to herself, pushing the rock out of the way, and noticed a pair of shoes lying on the ground. Turning over, Lainey rubbed her leg, making sure it did not hurt her, and reached for the shoe covered in dirt and hay.

"OMG!" Jessica screamed again; Lainey dropped the shoe, standing up to check on her friend, and saw her standing on a chair as mice ran across the floor.

"It's just a mouse, Jessica," Lainey said as Alison and Marnie rushed to them.

Alison bent over with her hands on her knees, trying to catch her breath. Marnie shook her head at Jessica.

"Someone kill it," Jessica yelled, twitching on the chair.

"Drama queen," Alison joked, waving her off.

Lainey picked up a piece of cardboard off the floor, nudging the mouse out of the way as Jessica jumped down from the chair and tried to hide behind Alison and Marnie.

"Where's the radio? Let's drink and dance," Alison suggested, taking the bookbag from Marnie's hold. Lainey tossed the cardboard down onto the floor, heading in the direction of the girls, when she paused. A feeling crept up in her mind that something was off about the shoe. Turning toward where she'd found it a few moments ago, she slowly stepped to the pile of hay stacked in the corner and saw not only a shoe but a jean jacket on the grate. Lainey lifted the coat up off the ground.

"What are you doing?" Jessica walked up near her.

"I saw this shoe and now a jacket."

"Somebody probably had sex in here, Lainey."

Jessica took the jacket out of Lainey's hand.

"You two are missing out on the fun," Alison said, passing Lainey a beer. Grabbing it out of her hand, she took a small sip as Jessica bent down to pick up the white Converse. Jessica walked further into the stall area.

"Maybe we should go," Lainey said.

"What are you so afraid of?" Marnie questioned.

1

New York-present

"Jessica! Jessica!"

"Huh?" She pushed her glasses up on the top of her head.

Coming out of her daze, thirty-two-year-old Jessica Smith always went back to that place of the summer months in Tennessee with her best friends in her younger days.

"Where did you go?" Ellen Sinclair, her staff editor at New York Gazette, lifted off the door and strolled into her office, planting her hands on the top of the chair.

"Thinking about being a kid again." Jessica threw the newspaper on the desk and turned in her chair.

"Have you given any thought to the case?" Ellen inquired.

"I have a lot on my plate right now." Jessica started to type on her computer, ignoring the questions. She grabbed the matcha green smoothie and sipped from the straw.

"I understand, but this could be your big break."

Jessica started to respond when her office phone rang,

interrupting her from having to answer. She held up her index finger for Ellen to hold on as she picked up the phone.

"Hello, this is Jessica Smith." She leaned back in her chair, getting comfortable.

"Jessica, I need your help," the voice whispered.

"Who is this?" Jessica picked up her pen, notepad, and sat up straight.

"I can't talk for long, but I think it's about the barn."

Jessica stiffened at the sound of that word being brought up. They'd agreed never to discuss what they saw that day, and now it was being brought to light.

"I don't know what you're talking about." Her eyes went up to look at Ellen, then down to the floor.

"It's me, Alison." The phone clicked, and Jessica pulled it away from her ear.

"Hello, Alison! Alison!" Jessica tried to redial the number, and the operator stated it was no longer in use.

"Who was that?" Ellen asked, stood up, crossed her arms, and peered at her.

"A friend."

"Are they all right?"

"I don't know. She sounded strange."

"Strange how?"

Jessica, not wanting to alarm Ellen, pushed away from the desk and grabbed her bags before turning the computer off.

"Where are you going?" Ellen questioned.

"I have a lead I need to follow up on, then I have dinner with my mom," Jessica replied. Then she slid her arms in her black trench coat, untucked her hair from the jacket, and picked up her keys and purse. Jessica Smith had grown up to be a beautiful woman. Some people thought she should be a model with her five-eight height and slim, athletic build. She loved fashion and the latest designs, and even though she'd gone to school for journalism, she dabbled in sewing and creating designs after learning from her grandmother. Jessica's brown skin popped against the purple turtleneck, her full lips coated in the latest Fenty beauty makeup. She topped off her medium-brown eyes with a little mascara, rouge on her high cheekbones, and locked her door. Ellen walked alongside her toward the elevator.

"Is the lead about the oil pipe story?"

Jessica pushed the buttons on the elevator and nodded her head, distracted by the phone call she'd just received and having to meet a deadline she knew was impossible. The elevator doors finally opened, and she stepped on, when Ellen held her hand out to block them from closing.

"Are you sure you're fine? You seem distracted."

Jessica put on a smile that didn't meet her eyes. "Ellen, stop worrying. I'm good."

"All right, but have that story on my desk by the end of the week."

She walked away. Jessica pressed the button for the main lobby again, and checked the time on her watch. Two-thirty.

She exited the building moments later, noticing cabs parked all along the front of the building. New York was her home away from home. When she'd told her parents about moving to explore her career goals, they'd been apprehensive but didn't stop her from the move. She had an apartment in Chelsea, which she loved, even though she had to work extra hours when she wanted to do certain things. Being a journalist wasn't the richest job in the world like people thought. She tapped on the window, and the cab driver rolled it down.

"Where to, ma'am?"

"Can you take me to West Central Park?"

"Yeah, hop inside."

"Thanks."

Jessica felt she should go check in on Alison before starting work on the oil spill case since all of her leads had dried up. She opened the door, slid inside, and buckled her seatbelt as the driver turned on the Left-hand and pulled into traffic.

"Music?" he asked.

"Doesn't matter."

She pulled out her phone and dialed Alison's number, and it went straight to voicemail. Even though she hadn't spoken to her in a few weeks, they were extremely close. All of her friends kept in touch if they needed anything. Jessica could admit sometimes she blew off girls' nights to work when she was close to breaking a lead, but overall she made it a priority to spend time with everyone.

Alison was always into some type of drama. She wanted to be an actress and went out on a few auditions, but nothing had really taken off for her. She had a habit of dating rich men and letting them take care of her, but Jessica said she would never judge her friend even though she had different opinions on working to build your own. Thirty minutes later, the cab arrived near Alison's apartment building on West Fifty-first Street, and all she saw were ambulances and police cars. Jessica took money out of her pocket and passed it to the cab driver, then hopped out and ran toward the building, but she was stopped.

"No one can come in, ma'am," the officer said.

"What's going on?" Jessica watched the reporters clamoring to get set up, and the doors opened as a body was being pushed out in a black bag from the morgue, which she knew of too well, being in her field.

"I can't answer that. Do you live here?" he asked.

Jessica shook her head.

"Then you'll have to leave."

"But my sister lives here!" Jessica lied, knowing that would get her a chance to snoop around Alison's apartment without being questioned.

His eyes narrowed in suspicion.

"Who's your sister?"

"Tommy, let her through," a deep raspy voice said from behind him.

Tommy looked over his shoulder, nodded at Detective Leo Walsh, and removed his arms from her elbow to let her pass through. Detective Walsh was around six feet two, with broad shoulders, full lips, dreads pulled back into a ponytail, dark brown skin, a full beard, and dimples in both of his cheeks. He'd hurt his knee in college and decided basketball wouldn't be his end goal. Instead, he went into criminal justice and became a police officer, working his way up to detective at thirty-five years old.

"What's going on, Leo?" Jessica had known Leo for the past few years since she'd been newly hired at the Gazette. When she needed answers on a story and he was the detective working the case, they often clashed. He admired her gutsy and feisty attitude when she went up against other people, but it drove him crazy when she brought the same energy on him.

Everyone thought that Jessica and Leo were sleeping together, but that couldn't be further from the truth. Jessica never mixed business and personal life. Leo was an extremely handsome man, but she would never cross the line and let people think she only got stories because she'd lain on her back. Leo knew this was going to be tough because Jessica talked to him often about her childhood and growing up during the summers on a farm with her best friends.

"I need you to keep this between us and be calm when I tell you."

Jessica's brows scrunched into confusion.

"What is it?"

He looked around the lobby, down into her eyes, and sighed. This was going to break her heart, and he had no choice but to tell her before the story ran on the six o'clock news.

"Alison is dead."

Jessica backed away from him, shaking her head, tears pooling in her eyes.

"Where is she?"

"I'm sorry, Jessica. I got the call, and they thought it would be best if I handled the case."

"I need to see her." Jessica tried to move around him, toward the elevator to Alison's apartment.

"They're wrapping up upstairs. You can't go right now."

"You have to be mistaken."

"I wish I was, but it's her."

"No, she just called me."

"When... Today? How long ago?" Leo took his notepad and pen out of his side pocket.

"Less than an hour, I think, maybe less."

"What did she say?"

"I...I...can't remember exactly." Jessica was hesitant to spill any details until she saw Alison for herself. Leo was a friend, but he was still a cop, and she didn't want anything keeping her from finding out the truth and getting the person that had done this to her friend.

Leo, grasping both sides of her arms, forced her to look

up into his eyes, when the elevator doors closed behind them.

"Jessica, I'm on your side."

"I know."

"Do you? I feel like you're shutting me out."

"No, I just can't believe that she's gone. Are you positive?"

The doors opened again, and two more officers walked out with bags of items in their hands. Jessica stared and noticed the friendship bracelet that all four of them wore as a promise when they were younger.

"Oh my God!" Jessica snatched the bag out of his hands.

"Hey! That's police evidence."

"Jessica!" Leo called out and took the clear plastic bag back.

"You can't take the bracelet. Please, Leo," Jessica pleaded, watching him hold the bag up.

"Leo, that's evidence," Officer Ritcher said, ignoring Jessica's pleading.

"Once they check for fingerprints, I'll get it back, okay?" Leo told her, and she wiped the tears from her cheek.

"Can I go upstairs?"

"I think you need to go home, Jess. It's not the best time."

"I won't touch anything. I just need to see it for myself."

"You're too close to this, Jessica."

"You're right. I'll wait a few days and then come back." She turned to walk off, scanning the small crowd that stood outside. Taking the opportunity of the police being distracted, she slipped to the back alley and went to the side exit door that was left unlocked, slipped through it, and went to the stairs. No one was around, so she ran up the stairs to the fifth floor and peeked through the doors, seeing the officers leaving and locking up the apartment. Jessica remembered that Alison had left an emergency key with her, which she hadn't used in months. She slid her hand in the purse and lifted it from the key chain, pushing the emergency door open. Strolling to Alison's door, she slid the key in, and unlocked it. Slowly, she kept her eyes closed to help contain her emotions and felt a cold chill ran up her spine. Slowly opening her eyes, she gasped. This wasn't normal for Alison's apartment. The place was trashed with papers on the floor, clothes thrown around, and the windows closed. Alison was a spoiled brat with semi-OCD, and she had a specific way about everything. Jessica planted her hand over her mouth when she saw the chalk outline of a dead body. Her tears started to come back, falling down her cheeks. More than anything, she was feeling regret for not keeping an eye on her friend and guilt that Alison felt she couldn't come and tell her if something was wrong.

"What happened, Alison?" she murmured to herself, strolled to the mail lying on the desk. She didn't want to touch anything, so she used her pen to move items around, seeing mostly bills and messages for auditions.

"Who did this to you?"

"I asked the same question."

Jessica jumped in shock, holding her hand to her chest. Leo closed the door behind him and pushed his hands into his pants pockets.

"You scared me."

His head tilted to the side at her comment. "What did I say?"

"Leo."

"No, Jess. This is a crime scene."

"I get that, but she's my best friend!" Jessica shouted.

"Keep your voice down."

"I...I... You wouldn't understand," she stuttered, pacing

in front of the desk. Alison lived in a two-bedroom, two-bath apartment with high ceilings and tall windows that looked out over Central Park. Its plush living room and bedroom looked like they cost more than Jessica's entire apartment. If her friend was into something serious and she'd missed the signs, she would carry the guilt forever.

"Try me."

"Did you get anything from her cellphone?" Jessica changed the subject.

"You're not working this case."

"Leo, my best friend was killed and you don't—"

"Who said anything about it being a homicide?"

"She wasn't sick."

"Could have been an accident."

"I want in on this case."

"You're a reporter."

"Which means I have a right to know who killed my friend."

"You do. Only when the case is solved, not during the solving."

"That's—"

"Look, Jess, I'm not arguing with you about the details. Go home and relax." Leo reached for the door handle.

"How is that supposed to happen when I was the last person to talk to her?"

"What did she say?" he questioned, his left brow rising.

Jessica glanced around the apartment, not making eye contact when she noticed a brown booklet on the couch in the corner.

"Is that her neighbor?" Jessica pointed at the door, and when Leo turned, she reached down and grabbed the note-book and pushed it into her purse. He turned back around, looking at her suspiciously.

"Be honest with me, Jessica." Leo ushered Jessica out of the apartment, locking the door behind her.

"Of course, Leo. I want her killer found, and I can help."

"You write stories about business and charity events."

"That doesn't mean I can't help you in this case."

"Go home."

"Keep me updated."

Jessica tried hard to not roll her eyes at being ignored, but she decided to take his advice and go home, but do some of her own investigating into things. If Alison's death goes unpunished, she'd never forgive herself as a journalist or friend.

2

Jessica peeled her jacket off once she arrived home and dropped it on the couch, kicking off her shoes. The cab ride back to her apartment was exhausting with the afternoon traffic and people yelling and screaming to get out of the way. She wished she could have talked to Alison sooner, maybe even earlier on the phone and told Ellen to leave her office. Once the door was locked, she went to the kitchen and grabbed a bottle of wine, deciding to order dinner to be delivered since she wasn't up for cooking. Her appetite was gone, but she needed to keep her energy up in order to make some phone calls and figure out what had happened to her friend. After pouring herself a glass of wine, she took out her cellphone and the notebook and sat on the couch Jessica had missed calls on her phone and never noticed it was on silent.

"Shit." She went to her voice messages, thinking some clue might have possibly been left by Alison. She pushed the button and heard her mom's voice.

"Hey love, call me when you get this message."

She switched to the next voice message by Ellen.

"Jess, I heard about your friend. It's all over the news. Take some time if you need to."

Jessica blew out a breath. "What happened to you, Alison?" she blurted out.

Feeling sick to her stomach, she called her mother while her mind kept drifting to the Summertime with her friends in her grandparents' hometown.

"Jessica, I'm so glad you called."

"Hey, Mom."

"Why do you sound down, honey?"

She sighed, debating whether she should tell her parents.

"Alison was killed."

A loud gasp was heard through the phone.

"Alison your friend?" she questioned.

Her eyes closed, then opened as a tear rolled down her cheek.

"Yeah." She cleared her throat.

"How? I mean, did they catch who did it?"

"No, all I know is that she tried to call me earlier."

"Ohh, honey, I'm sorry. What do you need me to do?"

"Nothing right now."

"I was calling to see if you're coming to visit."

"Uhm, I doubt I'm in the mood."

"Your grandparents would love to see you."

"How is everyone?"

"Doing good and all they do is talk about you in the big city."

"Maybe when we get a lead on Alison's case."

"Don't stress yourself out."

"I can't promise that."

"Alison was a sweet girl, all of your friends."

"Mom."

"Yes?"

"You remember that day?"

"That's something I wish you hadn't seen, baby."

"We promised to never talk about it again, but lately it's been running over and over."

"It's traumatizing for a child, and maybe it's time to talk to someone."

"Where's Dad?" She changed the subject, like her mother knew she would when things branched off into her having to speak with a professional about that day.

"Watching his sports, honey."

"Well, give him a kiss for me and tell everyone I said hello."

"Think about coming to visit, Jessica."

"I will, love you."

"I love you more."

Jessica ended the call and stared at the phone.

Knock!

Jessica stood from the couch and headed to the door, pulled money out of her pocket for the delivery driver and thanked him with a big tip. The elevator doors opened and her neighbor stepped off with his dog that she loved babysitting. The delivery driver stepped on before the doors closed.

"Hi, Alex."

"Sorry about your friend. We're you two really close?" Alex questioned as Jessica bent down and patted his dog's head. She released a breath, stood up.

"Best friends, just heartbreaking."

"If you ever need to talk, I'm here." Alex extended an arm out for a hug.

"Thanks, let me get inside and eat before my food gets cold."

"Have a good night, Jess." Alex waved goodbye, heading down the hall to his apartment. She closed the door, stood with her back to the wall, tears stung at her eyes, and mumbled a prayer. Jessica was determined to figure out what happened to Alison, even if that meant hounding the police even more than usual.

THE NEXT MORNING, Jessica stood outside of Leo's office holding two cups of coffee and tapping lightly on the door.

"Come in!" he shouted. She shifted the knob and pushed it open, and he was on the phone with a grim look on his face. Smiling, she held up the coffee and went to place it on his desk, sitting across from him.

"Let me call you back, Simon." Leo clicked the top of the pen in his hand as Jessica stared around the room at his awards and plaques.

"All right, send it over now." Leo hung the phone up.

"Morning," Jessica said, sipping on her cup.

Leo leaned back in the chair and stared at her.

"What are you doing here?"

"You told me to come."

"No I didn't."

"Well, it's my best friend, and if you want me to not go it alone, then—"

"You're blackmailing me into letting you on this case."

"What? Leo, you make it sound devious. I want the bastard caught."

"We will catch them."

"I can't sit at home and wait. You didn't hear the nervousness in her voice."

"I'm sorry, Jessica, but you can't be on this case. You're too close to the victim, and you're not a cop."

"I won't be involved, just informed."

"Don't you have a job?"

Knock!

The door opened, and Officer William came inside with a stack of folders, which he passed to Leo.

"Thanks, Willy."

"Sure, no problem."

"What's that?" Jessica pointed at the folders, and Leo shook his head.

"Work."

"Leo, please."

"I have reason to believe Alison isn't the only victim."

"You mean like a serial killer?"

"I can't say."

"Yes you can."

Leo leaned forward, planted his elbows on the desk, and clasped his hands together.

"First, what do you know?"

"About?" Her gaze darted toward the folders, then to him.

"Alison, her life, everything."

"She told me she was doing acting."

"What has she been in recently?"

Jessica couldn't say, since she'd been busy with work. Her friends had wanted to catch up, but she put them off for the past few weeks, and now she regretted not answering their calls.

"I haven't been the best friend lately." Jessica drank more of her coffee as Leo dropped the files and typed on his computer.

"From what I gathered, this case matched another case back in Tennessee."

Jessica shifted in her seat uncomfortably.

"What do you mean?"

"At least three other cases came up in a database that match Alison's murder."

"The same manner of death?"

Leo couldn't go further and explain that DNA analysis had come up empty, that would put the whole precinct in a negative light because of the budget cuts when it came to these types of cases.

"Are you heading to work?" he asked.

Their eyes connected for a moment before she nodded.

"Go to work, and I'll call you if I come across anything." Leo dismissed her, and she rose out of her seat, tapped the file folder on his desk, and glanced at him.

"She's family, Leo."

"I gotcha, Jess."

Jessica gave a light smile, turned, and went out of his office to head to work.

3

He promised himself to leave things alone and not continue down the path of killing again. It was fifteen years later, his secrets were going to be exposed to the world, and that craving of watching the last breath leave a body had come back. He needed to figure out more alternatives to killing. In his late forties, almost fifty years old, he'd made a life for himself taking over his family's local plumbing and shower business. He was a simple man, five feet nine, quiet, with short, spiky, blond hair, a round belly, a thin mustache, round face, and square jawline. Most people said he blended in with the crowd, never causing an uproar, someone who loved his family and dogs. Living in Jersey in his family's home and commuting to the city for work was the highlight of his week when he met a pretty woman. Back in his youth, he had been shy and quiet unless his friends coached him on how to approach a woman. But what he liked to do was be in control, and he found that paying for company was the easiest thing rather than trying to date and put yourself out into the world and make a fool of yourself.

"Did you get the new wrench I wanted?" Bobby, one of his usual customers, pushed his basket on top of the counter. Connor removed, from underneath the inside compartment of the counter, a wrench that was labeled for Bobby.

"The new wrench is here and ready."

Connor gave a light smile.

"I've been waiting to put together my new TV stand with this beauty." Bobby grinned, showcasing his missing front tooth.

Ding!

Connor looked up at an older couple that walked into his shop. They reminded him of his parents.

"How are your parents doing?"

He rang up his wrench, glue, and tape. Bobby slid forty dollars on the counter, and Connor picked it up and typed in the amount. The register opened.

"Retired." Connor wasn't much of a talker unless it pertained to books, specifically history and Sci-Fi, his favorite genres to read. Connor bagged up Bobby's items and passed him the bag to leave, just as a young woman approached his counter.

"Excuse me, do you know where the plungers are?" she asked.

Connor froze. He held his hands at his side, rubbed them against his pants and stared at the young beautiful woman.

"Hello?" She waved her hand in his face.

"Sorry. There over on the second aisle." Connor pointed at the section for the bathroom.

"Thanks." Her pointed fingernail tapped on the counter before she shifted to her right and headed over to grab what she needed.

THE AFTERNOON RUSH came and went, so Connor closed up early, turned all the lights off, and walked to his blue two-door truck, slid his work bag in the back, and hopped in the driver's seat. All he'd had was a club sandwich and root beer, so his stomach was ready for a full meal. Something he'd love to have had is a home-cooked meal. He considered eating out at a restaurant, but his awareness in staring would show, and people would whisper, so he decided to stop at the grocery store and pick up some items to make dinner. After he drove for ten minutes, he stopped at the nearest store to his place, turned into the parking lot, and slipped the keys out of the Ignition, and ran over in his head what he needed for dinner.

"Pasta sauce, noodles, beef strips."

Heading inside, Connor picked up a basket, went down the first aisle, and grabbed a loaf of bread.

"Mushrooms."

"Oh sorry." She drew her hand back from the jar of sauce they both reached out for.

He stood frozen.

"I'll wait," she said, smiling at him.

Connor shook his head.

"Great minds think alike," she joked, and he placed the jar in his basket and walked off.

She shrugged her shoulders at the weird interaction, extended her hand for another jar, and continued to shop down another aisle. The young woman placed her head-phones in her ear and scratched off her list. Grabbing his last item, he came up to the register five minutes later.. Two people in front gave him enough space to watch the beautiful brunette smile and laugh with the cashier in line. She was no more than five-six in height. Slim figure, full pouty lips, and high cheekbones. The cashier gave Connor his change, and he grabbed the two bags and followed in step but kept a distance behind her. Scanning the parking lot to see if anyone noticed them, he smiled and unlocked his car and climbed inside, putting his bags on the floor. Normally he'd arrange something at his hotel, but he was short on time and patience. As he followed her out of the parking lot, he jotted down her license plate.

"Great minds think alike," he whispered and went in the opposite direction.

Hours later, around midnight, she was stripped down on the bed in her home wearing only her underwear, eyes wide open and hair disheveled. Connor stood up, put his shirt back on, and looked around the bedroom. He noticed a picture of the young girl with an older woman and man that looked similar in the face. It was a two-story gray home in a quiet neighborhood not far from the city. Before he walked out, he opened the door and let her dog inside the bedroom. Then he jumped in his car and drove back home, with the window down and took in the fresh air.

"Beautiful."

She was his tenth victim over the years, but in his own eyes, he wasn't a bad man. Same as other men that saw gorgeous women and felt a connection that became obsession eventually to where he had to kill them.

~

"WE HAVE another young woman found dead," the reporter said during the breaking news. Connor stood in his store taking inventory of items while the screen talked about the death of Molly Collins, a dental assistant who hadn't shown up to work and whose boss had sent friends to check up on her.

"Such a shame," Bobby commented on the TV.

"What's a shame?"

Connor's back was to the screen.

"That young girl murdered."

"Uhmm."

Ding!

A group of guys entered the store in construction gear and hard hats.

"I tell my nieces to always carry mace," Bobby explained, throwing tape and glue on the counter.

"Never be too careful." Connor was ringing up the items when a flash of Alison's face came up.

"This is similar to the case of the other young woman that was killed in her home." Leo shoved the camera out of his face. Connor gritted his teeth and noticed standing on his left side a familiar face.

"She's beautiful."

"What's that?" Bobby questioned, cupping his ear.

Connor looked from the TV to Bobby.

"Nothing."

He hadn't seen Jessica in years, but he knew she lived in the city. It would be harder to kill Jessica the way he did Alison because he knew being in the public light as a journalist would bring suspension. Family and friends had no clue of Alison's lifestyle as an escort. If they had stayed out of the barn that day, he wouldn't have done what he did to Alison, and now it only triggered him to go back into that place he'd tried to leave alone for a while. None of his victims ever compared to his first, but Connor fed the hunger that ramped up in his chest. Once that feeling of satisfaction came, he'd go back to being the quiet, unassuming Connor Little from the small town in Tennessee.

4

Two days later

Jessica slammed the phone down on the desk and rubbed her temples. A second victim was all in the news, and Alison's parents were in town to take her body home for the funeral. She'd promised to meet them at the hotel before they left today. Her boss had put pressure on her to do her job and let her personal feelings be put on the Back burner.

"You look like shit." Ellen stepped into her office.

None of the women she'd read up on had a record, so the patterns of what they had in common came down to being single, attractive, and trusting. Except for the last victim, police said the window was broken into, and the suspect got in that way.

"I have to meet Alison's parents later today."

"How are they holding up?"

"Not good."

"Maybe you need time off."

"I have to go talk to the ME." Jessica slid her arms in her jacket.

"How are you going to get them to talk to you?"

"Stanley's working today."

Stanley Mathers had had a crush on Jessica for a while, and she only went to him when her friend dated his brother-in-law and they met at a dinner. She picked up her purse, phone, and notepad and slipped them in her bag.

"Be careful. Whoever the person is that's doing this is progressing."

"I'll call you if I need your help."

Jessica hugged Ellen, left her office, walked down to the elevator, and pressed the button as the doors opened.

"Jessica!" someone called her name as she started to step on, and she looked over her shoulder.

"Yeah."

"Phone call," Ellen said.

"Tell them I'll call back."

"They said it's an emergency."

Jessica got off the elevator before the doors closed and stomped back to her office, extending her hand to grip the phone.

"Hello, this is Jessica Smith." The line was quiet, and she glanced up at Ellen.

"I remember you," a voice muttered through the phone.

Her brows rose in suspension.

"Who is this?"

"Alison was my favorite," he taunted, breathing heavily over the phone.

Jessica slid her hand in her pocket to grab her cellphone. She typed out to call Leo and held it up to Ellen.

"Why did you do it?"

"I'll see you soon, Jessica." The call ended, a worried look spread over their faces.

"What did he say?"

Ring!

She saw Leo's name scroll across and clicked to answer.

"Jessica, Ellen said it's an emergency."

"I...I..."

"Take a deep breath and tell me what happened."

Jessica sniffed and tried to get a handle on the call she'd just taken.

"He said Alison was his favorite."

"Anything else?"

She wondered how much Leo found out about Alison and if it would get out in the news and to her parents.

"I'm supposed to meet with her parents today."

"Can we meet up later?"

"Yes."

"Jessica."

"Yes?"

"We're going to get this guy."

"Thanks, Leo."

She clicked out of the call and sent a text message on her group thread, then jumped up to leave again.

HALF AN HOUR LATER, Jessica held a root beer float, burger, and fries in her hand while she stood at Stanley's desk.

"No, Jessica."

He wasn't the hottest guy in the world, but he had a cute, quirky way about him that Jessica found amusing. He stood around the same height, with reddish-brown skin tone, a thin nose, a Low-cut fade, and a beard.

"Stanley, you don't want my gift?"

Stanley stared at the food, then grabbed it out of her hands.

"Thanks."

"You're welcome." Jessica scooted on the edge of his desk and reached down at the papers scattered around.

"What are you doing here?"

"I need a favor from you, Stanley."

"No."

Stanley picked up the burger out of the bag, unwrapped it, and took a large bite.

"You don't even know what I was going to ask."

He removed the folder out of her way.

"I would get in trouble if I helped you."

"Come on, Stanley, we're friends. A little info, and I promise to not say anything."

"This burger is good."

She squinted her eyes. "Please, and I'll bring you another burger and fries."

"How about a date?"

She grinned and stood up from his desk. "Tell me about the case of Alison and the Molly girl."

He stood up, walked to his door, shut it, and slid his hands in his pockets, his brows dipped low.

"Strangled, no physical evidence of clothes beyond underwear."

"Did he use a condom?" Sorrow shot through her heart.

A wry look scanned his face, and he soothed a palm down her arm.

"I'm sorry, Jessica."

"Thanks, Stanley."

Jessica walked out of his office despairing at being no closer to finding out who did this to Alison. Her stomach twisted in knots as she left the building and heard her phone ring.

"Jessica."

"Hey, did you find anything out with Stanley?" Ellen questioned.

"No, I'm headed to meet Alison's parents now."

"No one would fault you if you needed time off."

"Not until we catch this guy."

"You're not a cop, Jessica. Let them handle him."

The way he'd left her body like she was nothing and didn't mean anything to her family and friends drove a fire in her belly to look the killer in his eyes when he was captured to give peace to Alison's family.

"I'll call you later," Ellen protested as she clicked out of the call and slid the phone in her pocket, and left.

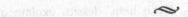

HER HEART THUMPED as she raised her hand to the door and knocked once, then twice. The door opened to a woman she'd known all her life. Her beauty still showed, even though she'd recently hit fifty-five years old. The short blonde bob and light streaks of gray blended over the top as she held back the tears from streaming down her face.

"Oh, Jessica." Tonya reached her arms out for a hug, and Jessica closed the space between them.

"So sorry for everything."

"It's not your fault. Alison walked down her path alone." Tonya stepped to the side and let her in the room. Jessica scanned the room and noticed Alison's father on the phone and other people in the room she hadn't met before. The door closed, and Tonya motioned for Jessica to sit on the couch.

"What can I do to help?" Jessica asked.

"You just being here is enough, Jess. Alison loved you and the other girls." Tonya's palm covered Jessica's, then she picked up a photograph of the girls all hugged up together one summer in front of their house.

"You remember how you four stayed running off for hours at the barn?" Tonya chuckled, running her hand across the frame of the photo.

"Alison was the leader," Jessica recalled, laughing to herself.

"Was she really making it as an actress? Be honest."

Jessica hesitated for a moment. Her loyalty to Alison was undeniable, but she didn't want to lie to her parents.

"That was the ME's office, they'll release her body to us soon." Paul took a seat next to Tonya and placed his arm around her shoulder.

"If you need anything, I can help," Jessica explained again.

"Once we get her home, we'll let you know the funeral information," he replied.

"I do have a question for you if you don't mind."

Tonya picked the napkin up off the table and wiped her tears.

"What kind of questions?" Tonya probed.

"I know you've talked to the police, but I was curious if Alison said anything about who she was dating."

Paul shook his head.

"Alison kept her love life private." Paul informed.

"Have you seen her lately?" Tonya pressed.

"No. Actually, I haven't hung out with any of the girls in a few months." Jessica confessed, clasped her hands together.

"You four were the best of friends. Don't let time or distance get in the way," Tonya remarked.

"I won't." Jessica answered.

"Are you hungry? We ordered room service."

"No thank you. I have to get going, but please keep me

updated on the funeral arrangements." Jessica stood up, and Tonya and Paul also rose from the couch.

"We still live in the same home, so you can reach us anytime." Tonya extended her arms and pulled Jessica in close.

Jessica walked to the door, which she opened right as room service approached.

"You can set it right over in the corner," Paul said.

Tonya held the picture in her hand for Jessica.

"Take this, Jessica."

"I wouldn't feel right taking your picture."

"I want you to have it, and besides, I know you're going to catch whoever hurt Alison."

Jessica took a few minutes to think it over before she grabbed it from her hand and hugged them both one more time before leaving the hotel room and going back home.

5

Three days later

He swallowed the sip of coffee, tossed the empty cup in the trash can, scanned the area, put his hands in his pockets, and jogged over to the apartment building he'd been watching for the last few days. After he'd reached out to his parents, he'd found out Alison's parents had flown her body back home and the funeral was coming up. He inquired about Jessica, followed her work schedule, and found her address. Today he'd had a coworker open the shop while he was out. He'd already had two victims, so he needed to hold off from being messy and adding another until things cooled down. But the goal was to shut Jessica up, and the other two friends that had seen him that day. This would only cause problems for his parents back home if they found out their son killed people and had a desire to cause pain to women that rejected him. Before he could reach her door, he noticed Jessica and Leo walk out of her apartment building. He slid behind a wall, watching them step into the car and pull off. He ran back across the street and jumped in his truck, following them down the street to where they were stopped at a light.

"Ring!"

The light changed, and he continued to stay two cars behind at a steady pace when they turned down a street and drove for another mile and ended up at the hotel he'd frequented with Alison.

"Shit!

"Ring!

He snapped up his phone and answered.

"What?"

"Mr. Little, the inventory of paint came in, and you told me to call," Tony said.

"Thanks. I'll be there in a minute."

He watched them get out of the car and walk in. As he turned into traffic, Jessica glanced over her shoulder, and they made eye contact.

"We'll meet soon."

Connor arrived twenty minutes later at the shop, parked, turned the car off, and jumped out, carrying his work bag.

"Mr. Little." Tony finished ringing up a customer.

Connor walked into his office and dropped his bag on the floor, turning the computer on. That was one of the things he updated when he took over his family's business. Being more modern made the workload easier and cut the long hours in half.

"Yeah, Tony?"

"Here's the list of inventory." Tony dropped the papers on his desk.

"You can take your break."

"Are you sure?" Tony looked down at his watch.

"Is it busy today?"

"No calls and only two or three people came for parts," Tony answered.

"Then you can go on your lunch break and put the closed for lunch sign out."

Tony nodded and turned to leave his office. Connor found the hotel's website and called the front desk.

"Regency Hotel, how may I help you?" the clerk said.

"Yes, can you tell me why the police were at your hotel today?"

"I'm sorry?"

"As a guest of your establishment, I'm concerned a crime has taken place."

"Well, I can assure you nothing has taken place at our hotel. We just had routine questions about a former guest."

"Are they on the same floor as me? Maybe I should check out."

"Oh no, sir. They just wanted to know if she was here recently, that's all."

The clerk rambled off, not adhering to the rules of giving out confidential information.

"Well, I hope it has nothing to do with those women being killed."

"That's the same thing I wondered since one of the girls came here frequently."

"Really? Which one?" Connor challenged.

"You didn't hear it from me, but the Alison girl was here a lot. I think she was a hooker."

"Interesting."

"Definitely. What was your name, sir? We can send you a free room service to make up for any concerns."

"That won't be necessary." Connor ended the call and pulled up the photos of all the girls. He marked Alison's name and smiled.

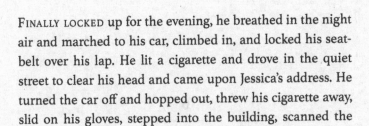

FINALLY LOCKED up for the evening, he breathed in the night air and marched to his car, climbed in, and locked his seatbelt over his lap. He lit a cigarette and drove in the quiet street to clear his head and came upon Jessica's address. He turned the car off and hopped out, threw his cigarette away, slid on his gloves, stepped into the building, scanned the mailboxes on the wall, and found her address.

"Do you need help finding someone?" A young man holding a trash bag in his hand walked into the lobby.

Connor kept his back to him and shook his head.

"Okay."

Connor waited a few minutes and turned toward the elevator as the young man continued down the hallway to the trash bin. He pushed the elevator doors closed and rode it up to her floor, tightening his gloves on his hands as the elevator stopped and the doors opened. He looked at the numbers on the doors and went to the apartment. He placed his hand on the knob and tried to open the door.

Ring!

"Shit!" He ran off down the hall to the exit doors and pulled the cell out of his pocket.

His alarm had gone off at the store.

"Hello."

"Mr. Little, we got a call about your alarm going off."

"That's fine. It's just some kids playing around like usual."

"Yes. Sir. Do you want us to drive over and see?"

"No. I'll take care of it myself."

Connor sighed, dropped the phone back in his pocket, left the building, and jogged to his car to drive back to the store.

6

Knock! Knock!
The early morning arrived, and Jessica squeezed the pillow around her head to block out the noise from whoever was trying to get her attention.

"Jessica! Jessica!" Leo yelled, knocking again on the door.

"What, Leo?" Jessica yanked the door open, tightening her robe. He pushed a bag of donuts in her arms, along with a cup of coffee.

"Can I come inside?"

"Fine." Jessica gestured for him to come inside, then shut the door behind him. She walked to the kitchen, opened the bag of donuts, placed them on a tray, and went back to the livingroom and set them down.

"Why are you here at...eight am?" Jessica scanned the clock on the wall.

"I did some digging and wanted to ask you some questions."

"What questions?"

"Did Alison say who she was dating or where she met her men?"

"Besides the hotel we saw yesterday, I have no clue about Alison's love life."

"From what the front desk clerk stated, she met a lot of men there."

"An escort. I know." Jessica took a bite of a donut.

"We're getting the camera footage pulled."

"I want to see them."

"I was afraid you were going to ask."

"That's my job, Leo."

"How did it go with Alison's parents?"

She shrugged her shoulders. "As well as could be expected. Heartbroken."

"I can understand."

"Can I tell you something?"

Leo dropped the donut on the plate and sat back on the couch.

"Shoot."

"I'm sorry I didn't tell you this earlier. I guess I was afraid it would be true."

"Tell me."

"I think Alison's murder has something to do with my hometown."

"What do you mean?"

"When you said they looked in the database and nothing came up, I did a little digging."

"Of course you did."

Jessica stood up, went to her bedroom, grabbed the folder of the old case from her hometown, and dropped it on his lap.

"What's this?"

"When I was a kid, during the summer I used to stay with my grandparents."

"This is a crime file."

"A girl was killed, similar to Alison and the Molly girl."

"How did you get this?" Leo flipped through the photos of the dead girl.

"Not important, but the girl was killed when we were around thirteen or younger."

"You witnessed the killing?"

"We just saw the body."

"We?" he questioned.

"Me, Alison, and my other two best friends."

"What are you saying?"

"I think it's the same person."

His brows crinkled into a frown.

"That's not possible, Jessica."

"How do you know?"

"That's been over fifteen years, maybe twenty."

"The guy could still be alive and knows what we saw."

"I think you've been watching too many crime shows."

"Leo, listen to me."

"Jess, you're still upset about Alison and maybe letting that compromise an old case."

"Leo, I think he killed her."

"Who?"

"I don't know!" she yelled, dropped down in the chair.

Leo reached over and pulled her into his arms, rubbing her back.

"It's okay."

"I swear, Leo, something strange is going on."

"Get dressed and ride with me."

"To where?"

"We can get some real food and check out the photos from the hotel."

"Thanks."

"Go shower."

She pushed him in the shoulder and went to her bedroom.

An hour later, they left her apartment and went down the elevator, laughing.

"Hey, Jessica."

"Hey, Alex." She patted his dog on top of his head.

"Did your friend find you?"

"What friend?"

"The guy last night."

Jessica and Leo glanced at each other.

"What guy?"

"Some guy was here standing in front of the mailboxes, and I saw he was focused on yours. I assumed he was looking for you."

The hair on the back of her neck stood up.

"How did he look, Alex?"

"Older, maybe forties, not too tall, stocky," Alex explained.

"Thanks."

Leo held the door open, let her leave, released the locks on their doors, and they slid in and stared at each other.

"What are you thinking?"

"I think it's strange some guy came looking for me, right as we get closer to clues in Alison's death."

"You think he was following you?"

"Probably."

"Do you have to work?"

"In an hour or two."

"All right, let's go grab the photos and get something to eat."

They flipped through the menus as the waitress poured coffee in their cups.

"I'm Harriet, welcome to Edna's."

"Can I get a vegetable omelet and sausage on the side?"

"Yes, ma'am. Anything for you?"

Leo poured cream in his coffee and took a sip. "I'll get the same and add pancakes."

"Be right up."

When Harriet turned toward the employee entrance, Leo pulled the still photos out, placed them on the table, and flipped it open to Alison at the front desk.

"I had them focus on sending me the dates of Alison visits and men that showed up around that time."

He pushed the photos toward Jessica.

"That's her," Jessica said.

Ring!

Jessica scrolled over her phone and saw that it was Ellen calling.

"Ellen, can I call you back?"

"No, it's an emergency."

"What's goin' on?"

"They want to know when you are going to leave this case alone."

"This is important to me," Jessica whispered over the phone as Harriet laid both plates down on the table.

"I know, but they feel like you've taken too much time on these cases."

"That's bull."

"Are you coming in today?"

"Yeah." Jessica lifted her hand to check the time on her watch.

"All right, come see me as soon as possible."

"Thanks, Ellen."

Jessica dropped the phone on the table and rubbed her forehead.

"Work problems?"

Leo flipped the lid on the syrup and poured it over his pancakes.

"They want me to stop working on the case."

He didn't reply to her comment.

"You think I should."

"I agree with them."

"Leo."

He cut into his pancakes and took a bite. "Alison's case will get solved."

"I know."

"I wanted to ask you a favor."

"Another one?"

"Yeah, I have this gala I have to go to for charity."

"You need a date."

"It's not a date."

Jessica tapped her watch. "I need to get back to the office. Do you mind if I look over these photos?"

"Yes I mind. Do you recognize any of these men?"

Jessica pressed her lips together in a pout and scanned the four photos of men. Two of them looked like the same guy.

"No, I don't know any of them."

He closed the folder and picked up his fork to continue eating.

"I'll let you know what I find."

She rolled her eyes and slid out of the booth.

"Call me, Leo. I mean it."

"Remember I'm the cop, you're the journalist."

Jessica bent down to whisper in his ear and picked up a piece of his pancake, tossing it in her mouth.

"How can I ever forget?" She sauntered out of the diner and called for a car ride and went to the office. She paid the driver, shut the door, and ran into a large body.

"Oh, excuse me."

She smiled. "No, it's me being clumsy."

He didn't return her smile, just tipped his hat and continued on to his car. Jessica felt a little uneasy feeling but shook it off and went on to work.

7

J essica removed her jacket, hung it on the back of her
chair, picked up her pen and notepad, and sat down
in her desk

Knock!

"Hey." Ellen tapped on her office door.

"I'm here."

"He's in his office."

"Great."

"He's an ass."

"I know." She blew out a breath and turned her
computer on to print up the stories of the cases from back
home.

"Leo showed me the photos of Alison."

"Any updates?"

"No, but I told Leo about the killing back home."

"Is he going to look into whether there's a connection?"

"I don't know. He thinks I'm reaching."

"Trust your gut."

She typed in the information on Alison's death, then
clicked over to the old photos from the past.

"Hmmm."

"What?"

"I noticed all the women are faced the same when he kills them."

"So?"

"Well it could be nothing, or something that's intimate for him."

"True."

"Jessica!" a loud voice called out.

"He's on one."

Ellen watched as Jessica stood and picked up her notepad and pen to head to her boss's office.

"Shut the door," he said.

"Before you start—"

"Sit down."

"Chandler."

"Ellen is not in charge, you can't run to her," he said.

"I wasn't trying to avoid it."

"Why are you still on this case?"

Her brows dipped low in confusion.

"My friend was killed, Chandler."

"Have you met any of your deadlines?"

"No."

"Did you respond to any emails from potential stories?"

"No."

"Are you using your position at the police station to get information on this personal case?"

Her mouth opened, then closed.

"Jessica, I can understand this is sensitive for you, but you've been given enough leeway."

"What are you saying?"

"I need you to focus on other things."

"I..."

He blocked her from speaking.

"All I want is for you to go back to your office and work on what we pay you to work on. Is that clear?"

"Yes, very clear." Jessica rose from the chair, took the sheet off his desk, went back to her office, and read over the document about a local business stealing from their clients.

"How did it go?" Ellen questioned as Jessica entered the breakroom and opened the fridge, taking a bottle of water out.

"He wants me on some case about stolen funds."

She showed Ellen the form.

"Well, at least he didn't fire you."

"I guess."

Jessica waved at another coworker and went to her office, back to her desk. She'd just started to research the local business when an idea came into her mind. She put the story aside and went back to the case.

Ring!

"Jessica Smith."

"Finally you answer the phone," Marnie fussed.

"Hi."

"How are you?"

"Good. Still crazy to think about."

"We promised to always be friends," Marnie reminisced.

"Are you in town?"

"Not yet. Still have another month to go," Marnie responded. She worked as a traveling nurse. It was her life-long dream to not only travel but also to help people. Lainey lived in Townsend and was married with kids. Their lives had shifted from what they'd thought they would be when they were running around Townsend back in the summer.

"You're going to miss Alison's funeral."

"I have flowers being sent."

Beep!

An email popped up on Jessica's screen while she talked with Marnie. She clicked it open and saw a picture of a group of kids in summer standing in front of a barn.

"Marnie, let me call you back."

"What's wrong?"

"I don't know."

She put the phone on the receiver and zoomed in on the picture of the teenagers.

"Who is this from?"

She noticed the email was a fake @jakesnow123, so she went to Townsend's website and brought up the city's old records. Tapping into old high school records, she searched through the system's names of kids that graduated that year. Then she narrowed down to boys and clicked on photos to match against the emailed picture. She remembered that most of the teens had gone off to college right after the death of the young girl in the barn. Thinking back on how some of the guys had acted, she remembered one guy that seemed quiet unless pushed to do something.

The door swiftly opened, and Jessica pulled Leo in to have a seat on her couch. As soon as she'd had everything printed out, she'd come straight home and piled up all her research to get him to make an arrest.

"I was working, Jessica. This better be good."

"I know who killed Alison."

Jessica picked up the photo from the hotel and the printout of the email.

"Who?"

"A guy named Connor Little."

"Who is that?"

"Someone that hung around when I was younger in the same crowds."

"What makes you think he's the guy?" Leo scanned the other documents on the table.

Jessica pointed at the photo from the hotel.

"Even though he's wearing glasses and older, that build is the same, plus height."

"Jessica."

"Listen, Leo, the guy was always quiet, but weird. He'd stare at us but never say anything."

"So?"

"When we were younger, I told you we saw a dead body."

"You think he did the killing?"

"I know he did. Plus there was another killing in the same town, same way."

"I think you've been watching too many *Columbo* episodes or *CSI*."

"He lives here."

Leo shifted in his seat, looking up at Jessica.

"How do you know that?"

"Alex said someone was here looking for me. Alison and my other friends witnessed that murder years ago. What if he's here to kill us off?"

"That's a little overdramatic."

"Leo, please!"

"Sorry, but I can't lock someone up because you think it's him."

"He's around the age now—besides you even said other cases popped up similar."

"Which haven't been solved but happened in different cities."

"The guy has a plumbing business. He can move around easily." She threw her hands up in the air.

"What plausible reason is there for me bringing him in? Which I'm not doing."

"He sent this email, contacting Alison, and she probably recognized him after a few visits, and that's when he struck."

"I think that's farfetched.'

"I think you're not taking it seriously because it's coming from me."

Leo leaned back on the couch, staring at Jessica as she paced back and forth.

"Connor Little."

"Yes, I believe... No I swear he did the killing back when I was younger, and now he's doing it again and trying to kill me."

"Jessica, I would look like a fool if I brought this to the team."

"You'd look like a hero if we were right."

"I need more evidence and motive."

Jessica took out another document from her bag.

"Connor has never been married, his parents still live in town, and some gossip floating around says that the reason he's moved around is because he's aggressive with women."

"Where did you get this police report?"

"Don't ask."

"Jess!"

"Leo, are you going to help or not?"

"Trespassing, aggravated assault. They dropped the charges."

"Paid them off more than likely."

He ran a hand down his face. "I'll go ask a few questions."

"Great. I'm going with you."

"No."

"Yes." Jessica reached for her jacket.

"I thought you needed to get prepared for your trip."

"We still have two days before I leave for the funeral."

"I knew you would say that."

8

Leo lifted his badge as Tony rang up another customer at the register.

"How long have you worked here?"

"About a few months."

"How well do you know Connor?" Jessica questioned, and Leo rolled his eyes.

Tony shrugged his shoulders.

"We don't hang out like friends, but he's cool."

Jessica walked around the shop and picked up an item, then placed it back down. She saw an employee entrance in the back corner and glanced over her shoulder at Tony and Leo. Jessica touched the door, saw it was open, and slipped into an empty office. She noticed pictures on the wall of Connor and his family and a few of him when he was younger. She walked over to the desk, pulled the draws open, typed on his computer, and it popped on. She clicked around the screen and saw mostly work orders for the store and a few history lists of him searching porn websites.

"Gross."

She noticed an email account, and just as she started to click on it, the door opened.

"What are you doing?" Leo asked.

"I thought you were talking to Tony."

"He went to carry something out for a customer."

"All right, keep him busy."

"We don't have a warrant," he whispered, watching for Tony coming back in the store.

Ding!

"I'm coming." She clicked out of the email and ran back to Leo's side.

She closed the door and caught Tony talking to someone at the counter.

"When do you expect Connor?"

"I'm right here." He turned around and faced Leo and Jessica.

Jessica's eyes widened in surprise, remembering him from somewhere.

"Do I know you?" Connor questioned, stepping toward them. She backed up.

"I think we're from the same town in Tennessee."

"Are you Connor Little?" Leo probed.

"I am."

"These cops came to ask me some questions about the shop and you."

"What do you want to know?"

"Did you kill Alison?"

"Jessica." Leo groaned and planted his hands on his hips.

"I'm sorry, kill who?"

"Alison from our hometown."

"I think you have mistaken me."

"Townsend, Tennessee, around late early nineties during the summer."

His top lip curled into a smile briefly.

"Sorry. I don't remember you."

"Convenient."

"Sorry for interrupting you." Leo gripped her elbow, and they walked back to his car. He opened the door for her to get in and shut it behind her.

"What are you thinking?"

"He's the guy."

"Jessica, you know better than anyone that we need hard evidence."

"What do we do now?"

"I'll look into him further."

"What about having someone track him?"

"Let me do my job."

"Okay." Jessica crossed her arms over her chest, watching as Connor came out of his shop and stared at the car as Leo drove off down the street.

"That won't work."

He lifted a brow in her direction.

"What?"

"You're pouting in the corner. I won't let you jeopardize this case, Jessica."

She released her arms and cupped her face on the left side.

"Sorry, Leo."

"Remember I'm on your side." He tapped her palm with his index finger, and she nodded her head in agreement.

"Thanks, Leo." They drove for half an hour and made it to Molly's home to follow up on the witness's statement.

Leo wrote down the time and description of what the witness stated they saw from the night of Molly's killing.

Jessica kept her hands in her pockets. She wore gloves and a black knitted cap to help rein in her unruly hair. She stepped in close to the bedroom, but avoided compromising the scene, glancing down at the dog's bed and the discarded clothes on the floor. Her heart went out to the victim, and she wondered how her family was doing. The neighborhood was a quiet area, mostly families with kids. To have a murder was foreign to them, and they'd been on edge in wanting to catch the person before it happened again.

"So you told the investigators everything you know." Leo wrote in his notepad.

"Yes, Molly usually comes home around eight or nine," the older woman stated, lifting her glasses before they slid down.

"How long has Molly lived here?"

"I guess about three years, maybe five."

"Did you see anyone come and go lately, someone she's dating?"

"No, most of the time it's her friends that stop over."

"Miss Chambers, do you recall a guy driving a truck, maybe with a sign on the door?" Jessica queried.

"Mmmhm... I don't think so."

"That night can you recall anything strange?"

"Besides her dog making noise, that woke me up, and I came over to check on things."

"Does the dog bark late at night?"

"No, usually he's asleep."

"Okay, well if you think of anything else, here's my card." Leo reached into the side pocket of his jacket and removed a business card from his wallet.

"Sure, and hope you catch the bastard," she grumbled and walked out of the home to go back next door. Jessica and Leo stepped out and stared at the surrounding area.

"He's not stupid."

"I agree."

"He probably got cocky in thinking no one would put the killings together."

"I'm tempted to think you're becoming a cop, Jess."

"No, I'll leave that for you."

"When do you fly home?"

"Morning after next, why?"

"I might go with you."

"Really... What changed your mind?"

"The way Connor stayed even in tone when talking with you, plus the neighbor said someone was creeping around your place."

"You want to talk to Connor's family?"

"Yeah and the cops."

"He's probably not even shocked that we showed up."

"They never are."

They continued going house to house talking with neighbors to find out more information on Molly's killing.

***

Hours later, Jessica sat in her bedroom with her laptop open, eating leftover noodles, with files scattered across her bed. She wanted to at least try and do her normal job on top of figuring out Connor's mistakes. The local company that took money from clients was from upstate New York, and they'd been in business for over ten years.

"These numbers don't add up," she mumbled to herself.

Crash!

A loud crash was heard in the hallway of her building. Jessica removed her glasses, rose out of bed, grabbed her robe, and sauntered to the front door. She stood on her tiptoes looking through the peephole. She turned to look around her living area, turned her lights on, opened the front door, and looked down the hallway. It was completely empty except for some broken glass. She went to the window where the glass could have come from and noticed the side was broken.

"Kids." She bit her bottom lip, scanning the trail of the glass on the floor.

"Miss Jessica, I'll have someone clean this up soon as possible." The security doorman came off the elevator, talking into his headset.

"Thanks." Jessica went back into her apartment and shut the door. She went over to her phone and dialed Leo's number.

"Yeah?" he groggily answered.

"Sorry to bother you so late."

"Jess."

She stepped into her bedroom, pushed the computer to the side, and sat on the edge of the bed.

"I wouldn't be calling unless it's important."

"What's the matter?"

"It could be nothing, but I was up working and heard a loud crash and went to look."

"Are you hurt?"

"No, but it looked like someone broke a window in my building."

"I'm on my way."

"No, Leo, it's fine. The security team is cleaning everything up."

"Are you sure?"

"Yes, I just thought it was weird."

"If you need me to come over or have a cop do a walk through the area."

"I don't think it's that serious."

Jessica picked up her computer and shut it down for the night.

"Tomorrow I have a story to run that I've been avoiding."

"What's the story on?"

"Some corrupt business."

"That sounds more like your speed."

"It does, thanks, Leo."

"For what?"

"Keeping my mind distracted."

They both hung up at the same time, and Jessica crawled into bed with the thought of the broken glass on her mind.

9

S he listened to her boss talk about the latest stories they needed to be focused on, and Jessica could tell he was making it a point to look at her every time. Her building security had sent out a memo about the break-in that almost happened last night. He thought it was some kids playing that got out of hand.

"Jessica, what do you have?"

"The research is still coming in on my story."

"How much longer do you need? The deadline is close."

"Well as you know, Chandler, I've had an unexpected death of a friend."

All eyes went back and forth between Jessica and her boss.

"Should I give the story to someone else?" The expression in his eyes showed that he was challenging her to put the story on someone that was more eager and ready. He'd made it his goal to try to keep her in control, and Jessica had played by her own rules when it came to getting stories rather than be assigned a puff piece.

She tapped her pen on the conference desk.

"I have the time after I come back from the funeral."

"When are you going?"

"Tomorrow."

"Give Ellen whatever you have so at least she can keep me updated."

Ellen nodded her head at Chandler.

"Thank you for understanding, Chandler."

"Let me be clear: We have a mountain of stories waiting to be told."

Jessica shifted in her seat.

"I want us to be the first on scene and first to report. Do I make myself clear?"

Chandler scanned the room as each reporter stayed quiet.

"Good. I'll be in my office. Don't disturb me unless it's important." He walked out of the room.

Ellen and Jessica stood up, and she grabbed her notepad and research notes.

"You want to order lunch and work in my office?" Ellen queried.

"I guess he's going to be watching me now."

"Chandler's on an ego trip."

"He needs to get off my back."

Ellen wrapped her arm around Jessica and laughed as she walked into her office, pretending to mock Chandler.

"Okay, so where are you with the business case?" Her finger hovered over the keyboard.

"I got the records of the CEO's bank account." Jessica slouched down, grabbed the files, and held them out in front for Ellen to grasp. She flipped over the documents as her face scrunched up in confusion.

"What?"

"These numbers are off, but they seem to match up exactly to what they've spent in advertisements."

"That's strange."

"Big time. Thanks for bringing this to light, Jess."

"Just doing my job."

"I'm going to reach out and see if we can get a comment from the CEO."

"Doubt he'll agree."

"I know you won't be back in time, but I can send someone else."

Ellen put the papers on the desk, picked up her office phone, and dialed the number of another reporter. Jessica sat back and read through her notes on Connor Little until Ellen finished with her call.

Ring!

She dug her phone out of her pocket.

"Hi, Lainey."

"So sorry I didn't return your calls."

"I guess Marnie got in touch with you."

"She did. We'd been on a family trip."

"Are you still in Townsend?"

"We are, and I've spoken with Alison's parents to offer our help."

"I'm flying in tomorrow."

"Do they have any ideas of who did this?"

"No, but I have a feeling it's from the past."

"Jessica."

"Seriously, Lainey, there's no—" She paused and looked up at Ellen, who'd finished her call.

"Jessica."

"How are the kids?"

"Why'd you change the subject?"

"It's best if we talk in person."

"Sounds like you're hiding something."

"Give the kids a kiss for me and I'll see you soon." Jessica smiled, lightly laughed, and ended the call.

"I won't feel offended that you're hiding something." Ellen spoke.

"I'd rather not become the story, or my friends."

Ellen held her hands up in surrender.

"Jessica, we have a job to do."

"I'm doing my job." Her face hardened.

"You're leaving something out, and if Chandler finds out, you could lose your job."

"Can we finish this before it gets too late? I have to go home and pack."

"Jessica, you have a phone call." An older man with short, cropped hair and a medium build, walked into Ellen's office.

"Thanks David... Ellen, can we finish this later when I get back?"

Ellen waved her off and went to make another call.

"What's with the attitude?" David questioned.

"She's pissed I'm holding something on the serial killer case."

"What are you holding?" David stood at his cubicle as Jessica picked up the phone.

"Nothing."

Jessica clicked over and answered the call.

"This is Jessica Smith."

"You think you're smart," Connor taunted.

"I think you think that I'm smart." She snapped her finger at David for a pen and paper.

"I was close the other night."

"Close where, Connor?"

He chuckled, breathing hard on the phone.

"I like your apartment."

Her heart dropped at the mention of him going through her things.

"Is that right?"

"You've grown up, lovely Jess."

"I wish I could say the same, Connor."

"The four of you should have stayed out of the way."

"Are you threatening me, Connor?" Jessica held a note up for David to call Leo.

"Never threaten. I promise we will see each other very soon." Connor dropped the call, and Jessica clicked the receiver and dialed Lainey.

"*You've reached Lainey. I'm away from my phone. Please leave a message.*"

"Shit," Jessica mumbled and dialed Marnie's phone number.

"*This is Marnie. Nope, I'm not able to take your call, out saving lives.*"

She slammed the phone on the receiver and rushed toward her office to grab her coat, purse, and keys.

"Hey, I have Leo on the phone," David yelled as Jessica ran to the elevator.

"Tell him I'll call him back."

The thought of both her friends not answering caused her pulse to race and a migraine to start as her stomach got queasy.

THE CAB STOPPED RIGHT in front of her apartment, and she jumped out and rushed to the door as the security guard called her name.

"Jessica! You have a package."

Jessica pounded on the elevator button, and the guard ran over to pass her a package.

"Sorry, I'm in a hurry."

"Is everything all right?"

"No, not really." She took it out of his hands as the doors opened and stepped onto the elevator.

"Should I call someone, the police or a doctor?"

She waved him off. The doors closed, and she looked down at the wrapped gift. Not seeing a card, she removed the ribbon and ripped it open, and the elevator stopped on her floor. Jessica flipped it back over, and her heart dropped at photos of Marnie and Lainey individually with their faces crossed out by a red marker.

The pain of something happening to them because of her, ate at her conscience. She slid the key into her door, pushed through and slammed it, running toward the phone.

"Little Plumbing and Co. This is Tony."

"May I speak to Connor Little?"

"Sorry he's not in right now. Can I take a message?"

Jessica flipped the photos around to the back and front.

"Tell him I'm coming for him."

"What do you mean?"

"He'll know." She ended the call and dropped the photos on the table, rubbing her forehead.

"Marnie and Lainey."

Jessica stood up from the couch and went to the kitchen, opening the fridge to grab leftover salad, then a bottle of wine, and sat down in the loveseat, dialing Lainey and Marnie again.

"Hey, are you packed up?" Lainey answered the phone.

Jessica felt a load of relief and smiled.

"I will. Have you heard from Marnie?"

Jessica clicked back over from voicemail on Marnie's phone.

"No, last time we talked she had a patient."

"I called you earlier, but you didn't answer."

"My boys were playing with my phone. Worse than us when we were younger." Lainey laughed.

"How are they doing?"

"Good, just being bad as usual."

"You can't be mad. They take after you."

"Please, these kids think they pay bills around here."

"I can't wait to see everyone."

"We can't wait either."

"I'll let you go. I have to start packing."

"Call as soon as you touch down."

"I will. Bye, Lainey."

"Bye, Jess."

Ding!

"Who is it?" Jessica called out, stood, and marched to the door.

"Normal people wait for an answer," Leo replied as he closed the door behind him and followed Jessica to the couch.

"Normal is overrated."

Jessica picked up the pictures of Marnie and Lainey and handed them to Leo.

"What's this?"

"The reason we need to catch Connor now."

Although Leo knew deep down that Jessica was telling the truth, he couldn't go in and make an arrest without more evidence. He sat down and listened as she recalled the conversation and the information related to her from the phone call.

10

Townsend, Tennessee

He bagged up his clothes in a plastic bag, removed the last remnants of his belongings, and piled everything in the back of his truck. She was another fatal victim he had to dispose of before he moved on to the main ones on his list. He'd caught her when she was coming out of the local bakery a few stores down from the local market where he'd been shopping for his mother. He'd known Jessica would try and go to the store back in New York after he called and taunted her about her friends. Connor packed up and left Tony in charge while he came down to his family's hometown to finish off the job. His parents welcomed him with open arms and wanted to cook a big family dinner, so not only did he have a dead body to cover up, but groceries in the back of the truck. This wasn't a slow killing like normal; she had been a spur-of-the-moment thing, and now he'd have to try and clean up the cuts on his hands from her scratches before someone saw and questioned them. He covered the body with more trash in the barn and jogged back to the truck, scanned the area, and jumped in and drove back home. He wiped the blood that dripped down his cheek with a napkin and dropped it in his pocket to dispose of later. A few minutes later, he made it back home and grabbed the two bags from the backseat, shut the door, and walked up the steps, hearing yelling from the living room.

"He's home so we're going to celebrate!" his mother shouted.

"Pearl, don't you think it's strange he's come back after being gone over ten years?"

"No, that's our son, George."

The door slammed, and Connor glared at his father, marched toward the kitchen, and placed the bags on the counter. He hated that they hadn't stayed in Florida, but his uncle was sick, and his mother had come back to help him. So Connor had to play the doting son until they left, or try to suppress his thoughts of Jessica and the other girls.

"I won't be here long." He dropped the bags on the counter and started to walk out of the kitchen. His mother grabbed the bottom of his chin and turned it to the left and saw the scratch mark.

"What happened to you?"

"Nothing, Mom."

He jerked out of her hold.

"Stop treating him like a baby, Pearl."

"Stop telling me how to treat my son, George!" She slammed the kitchen towel on the counter, lifted the wooden spoon, and continued to cook the gravy.

"He's a man now. Treat him like one."

George lit another cigarette and opened the newspaper on the table. Connor stomped out of the room and up the stairs to his old bedroom.

Arriving in his room, he rushed to the closet, turned the

light on, pushed boxes aside, brought out a locked box, and placed it on his bed. He removed keys from his pocket and unlocked it, to find his memories of past women still safe where he'd left them. He'd cut a piece of hair from each woman he'd been with and saved them for posterity. To him, this was a goal and shrine for how accomplished he'd become in making them.

"What are you doing?" George asked, standing at his bedroom door.

Connor quickly shut the box, locked it, and jumped up to hide it back in the closet.

"You should knock before you come in here."

"What are you hiding, Connor?"

Connor stared at his father, then grinned. "Nothing, Dad, just a few memories."

His father chortled, puffing on his cigarette.

"Some dating, keepsakes"

"Something like that."

"I knew you had the dating magic, like your father." George stepped into his room and patted him on both shoulders.

"How long are you and Mom here?"

"Not long, her stupid brother hurt his back so we had to come back."

George walked to the wall of photos that held Connor's graduation.

"How are things in New York?"

"Great. I'm thinking of expanding the business."

"Where would you expand?"

He rubbed his chin.

"Maybe Florida. Tony's a great employee."

"Try to not work too hard and end up missing out on getting a wife."

Connor held his head down. "The women I date aren't interested in marriage."

"All women want marriage; you just need to show them who's the man." George tapped him on the chest.

"Yes, sir."

"Dinner! Come down here and eat," Pearl said.

"I don't know why you're here, but I don't want any trouble out of you Connor."

"I won't be here long."

MIDNIGHT FINALLY ARRIVED, and Connor left his family's home and slid in his truck and drove back out to the barn to try and get rid of the body. He drove down the small street that went from one end of town to the next and saw flashing lights surrounding the area. He knew a shortcut, and to avoid being seen, he turned off to the side of the road, passed through the rustic driveway a few yards from the barn, and parked the truck. Police and the local coroner were talking as photos were being taken of the scene.

"Fuck!" he groaned, watching as they brought a body out of the front of the barn. For being rushed, he'd had no time to really clean like he'd hoped. He started up his car and reversed out of the area and went back to the main road, stopped by a police officer, holding a flashlight and waving to him to roll down his window.

"Connor is that you?" The officer stood at the driver's side window of his car, one hand placed on the ceiling.

"Bill." Connor kept his hands low on the steering wheel.

"When did you get back here from the big old city?"

Connor scratched the back of his neck. "Today. I'm here helping my mom with my uncle."

"I heard about him hurting his back. A few of the guys helped to bring him groceries a few times."

"Surprised my mom let anyone help."

"You know Mrs. Little is stubborn."

They both chuckled.

"Try growing up with her. So what happened out here?"

"Well technically it's a police matter, and I can't talk about it, but you're a longtime Townsend. Some girl was killed out here."

"Wow."

"Brings up memories from the killings a few years back."

"It does."

"I can't believe they've never caught the guy."

"Hopefully with you on the force, something will change."

"Well, if they ever give me a chance to work a case."

"You're still on parking tickets?" Connor probed.

"Seven years doing the same boring thing."

Another police car pulled up.

"Bill! What are you doing?" The officer called.

"See, more crappy orders." Bill shook hands with Connor.

"I need to get back to the house."

"What were you doing out here?" Bill asked.

"I thought I forgot my phone earlier."

Honk!

"Come on, Bill!" the officer shouted.

"See you around, Connor!" Bill yelled and jogged back to his car.

Connor waved and drove by the cop car as the officer berated Bill. Ten minutes later, he parked back home, turned the car off, jogged back up the stairs, and unlocked the door. He was surprised to see his mother standing at the top of the stairs.

"Did you make sure it was clear?"

"Yes, Momma."

"Don't make any more mistakes, Connor." She turned and went back to bed.

He locked the front door and removed his jacket and gloves, headed upstairs, and saw his mom standing at the door of her bedroom. She nodded at him and shut the door once he went into the bedroom.

"LOCAL POLICE STATED she was a young girl around seventeen years old," the news reporter explained. Connor and his parents sat around the kitchen table the next morning and ate breakfast while the news played in the background.

"These kids nowadays," his dad muttered, flipping the newspaper over to the sports section.

"She's the daughter of Mariel Hanson, the clerk at Townsend real estate," Pearl commented, flipping over the pancake.

"She was probably out doing drugs." George slapped Connor on the shoulder.

"Whatever, George." Pearl pulled the pancakes out of the pan and placed two on each of their plates.

"*We have updated information. She was strangled and sexually assaulted*," the reporter stated.

"Are you helping Uncle today?" Connor questioned.

"Yeah, and you're going with me."

"I have work to do," Connor answered.

"What work?" Pearl barked.

"Work, Mother." Connor sipped the orange juice she'd poured.

"Let the boy go have fun, Pearl."

"Shut up, George. That's his problem now: no discipline."

George grunted and picked up his coffee, ignoring Pearl's complaints about his parenting. He took another sip and ate his food. Connor finished his and put his plate in the sink, kissing his mother goodbye.

11

J essica sat in the passenger seat worried sick. After getting frantic calls from her mother's friend, she had to come over and check on things. As the reporters lined up outside of the home she'd visited when she was younger, Jessica felt her stomach knot up. Her anxiety grew as the line of cars in front of the house covered the small cove.

"I know you're scared." Leo reached a hand to cover her palm.

Jessica turned from looking outside the window.

"Like I never left." She met his eyes.

Leo put the car in park and removed the key, and they both stepped out and walked through the crowd.

"Jessica! Jessica! Can you tell us anything about the case?" a reporter asked.

"No comment!" Leo barked, shoving a microphone out of his face.

The door opened, and her mother waved them inside. Jessica hugged her and stepped aside for Leo to reach his arm out for a hug. The room was filled with familiar faces, and she knew this was the worst possible position to be put in being so close to the case. Lainey held Mariel's hand, her mother sitting on the other end of the couch. Jessica made eye contact with Lainey who whispered in Mariel's ear before she stood up and met Jessica in the middle of the room for a hug.

"How is she holding up?"

"Not good."

"Is there somewhere we can talk?"

Lainey nudged her to the hallway.

"I got the call early this morning from my mom," Lainey explained, crossing her hands over her chest.

"My mom left early this morning to come here."

"Sick and twisted, Jessica."

"She was just a kid."

"Do you think it's him?"

"I know it's him."

"What do you want?"

"Me, you, and Marnie..." Jessica looked over her shoulder to see if anyone was listening.

"He's gone this long without trying to hurt us."

"I got too close and pushed the investigation on Alison."

"So that made him angry."

"Pissed is the better word. He tried to break into my apartment."

"Jessica, I have kids and a husband."

"I know, Lainey, and that's why you should leave here and get protection."

"What about moving to New York?" she fussed, throwing her hands up.

Jessica sunk her head.

"Marnie, Alison, you, and I all saw what he did in that barn."

"Why can't we forget what happened and move on?"

"Because he's killing more women."

"Jessica, Lainey, what's going on with you two?" Jessica's mother approached them.

They looked at each other, then her mother.

"We should tell her."

"No, Jessica, if it spreads, it will only cause bigger problems. Just go." Lainey started to walk off, but stopped and turned back toward them as Leo appeared in the living room.

"Who is that?" Lainey pointed at him.

Jessica shifted, looked behind Lainey, and motioned for Leo to come to the hallway.

"Leo is the detective working the case."

Leo extended a hand to shake, and Lainey and her mother greeted him.

"I've heard a lot about you, Leo. I feel we practically know everything about you," Lainey said.

"Jessica, you've been talking about me?" Leo joked.

"Leo, this is Lainey, one of my closet childhood friends and my mother, Mrs. Smith."

"Nice to meet you, Leo," her mother said.

"You as well."

"Did you find anything from the police?" Jessica inquired, glancing back to the living room.

"As you know, it's not my district, so I can't really get involved, but I did ask a few questions."

"What did they say?"

"She was supposed to stop at the store and go straight home."

"He kidnapped her."

"Her death was around seven or eight at night."

"He's getting bold."

"Who?" Mrs. Smith wondered.

"Mom, I never talked about this, but when we were younger we saw a dead body in the barn," Jessica explained. Her mother gasped and stumbled a little, but Leo caught her elbow.

"Why didn't you say anything, Jessica?"

"I was scared. We all thought he would come after us."

"You saw this too, Lainey?"

Lainey nodded, wiping tears that fell down her cheek.

"We all promised each other to never talk about it again."

"Did they ever catch the person?"

"No, but I know who's responsible."

"Who?" her mother queried, rubbing her arm.

"Connor Little."

"Little Plumbing Shop?"

"He knows we know," Jessica replied.

"Wait a minute. You're telling me a serial killer is here around us and you never told anyone?" she chastised.

"I didn't know how."

"Shirley, where's Shirley!" Mariel yelled. Shirley started to leave, but Jessica blocked her way.

"Mom, you can't tell Mariel."

"Why not?"

"He's probably here in town, and we need to get more evidence."

Shirley looked from Jessica to Leo.

"Is that true, Detective?" Shirley asked.

"Yes, ma'am."

"Oh dear God!" Shirley blew out a frustrated breath and went to sit near Mariel.

"What do we do now?" Lainey challenged, glaring at Leo.

"I'm going to go talk to Connor."

"You're not going by yourself."

"I can handle this, Jessica."

"Leo, either I come with you or I go by myself."

"What if he's not there?" Lainey investigated.

"Then I leave and go back to New York, and you continue to support your family friend," Leo told her. Lainey nodded, and all three started to leave the house. Jessica went to the passenger side of his car and waited for him to unlock the door.

"Stay out of the way, Jessica. I mean it this time," Leo growled.

"I'll let you handle the questions. What if we follow him for right now?"

"I'm not doing a stakeout with you in the car."

"I'm all you got."

"Do you know where he lives?"

"His parents are back from Florida, so we might end up talking to them."

"Why do you say that?"

"His parents are overbearing, especially his mom. His dad always tried to toughen him up, but she let him have leeway."

"Hopefully they're not home."

"Are you going to search the place?"

"If you can keep it between us, I'll let you help me."

"I'm sure I can keep this quiet."

AN HOUR LATER, they arrived at the home of Connor Little. It was midafternoon with no cars out front. Leo decided to park a few houses up to not be noticed and walk through the back to get inside. He picked the lock as Jessica kept watch on the neighbors. Most people were in town or shopping at this time.

"Remember, don't touch anything," Leo said.

They walked through the house, scanning the walls of family photos with Connor, his parents, and grandparents.

"Look at this." Jessica pointed to the kitchen, glancing at the newspaper and coffee pot half full.

"They'll probably be back soon. Let me check out the bedrooms." Leo went to look for the basement.

"I'll start upstairs," Jessica answered.

"No! Stay close by me."

"Leo, it would save more time if we split up."

Leo grappled with how to answer. He knew she would do it anyway, and wasting time in arguing would only cause more problems.

"No more than five minutes, Jess."

She gave him a thumbs-up.

"Hurry," Jessica whispered, and they split off. Leo ran to the side door of the kitchen and slowly opened it up. Pulling out his gun, he stalked through the basement and noticed only the laundry machine, clothes, and old furniture. He picked up a few of the empty boxes and looked over the old magazines of porn, cars, and guns.

"Family bonding," Leo muttered at the magazines addressed to Connor.

As he searched, Jessica opened the door of Connor's room, surprised by how cleanly it was set up with a bed, chair, dressers, and photos on the wall. She opened and closed drawers, not finding what she needed. She went to the closet, opened the door, and pushed the clothes back to rifle through the boxes. She grabbed an old high school binder, flicked it open, and saw names of people from school. Some she recognized and others she didn't, while she continued getting lost in the binder.

Connor watched from the door. After he left his parents at his uncle's place, he went back out to the barn and came home. He knew the neighbors weren't home, so the strange car had to be police. He grabbed the gun out of his father's room and slipped into the house undetected.

The lights flickered on, and she looked around the room, noticing she was surrounded by stacks of newspapers, books, and trash. All she remembered was that Leo had gotten a tip to come out to old Little's farmhouse that had been on sale for years. She didn't hang out too much with their son because he was older and often standoffish. Jessica stood up slowly, and almost fell back down from the weight of a major migraine. She reached for the back of her head and felt a large knot.

"Mmmm."

She pushed the papers on the desk and saw stories of young women missing, all ages, races, and sizes. She scanned the room that held only a chair, bed, desk, and wall plastered with newspaper clippings. Stepping forward and hearing a creak in the floor, she swallowed the lump in her throat and continued to the door, gripped the knob and twisted it until it opened. She slowly looked left, then right down the hall to see if anyone was around. Jessica's eyes narrowed into thin lines as she walked down each stair and glanced around the room of the home she wasn't familiar with, besides having ridden her bike past it every summer when she was younger.

"Leo!" she whispered and ran toward the front door. As she tried to remove the lock, she heard a laugh and froze in place.

"I'm glad you came."

Jessica released a breath and turned her head to see Connor Little standing in the hallway with a gun in his hands.

"Connor."

"Jessica, you look more beautiful than you did at thirteen."

Her body shivered at the thought of him calling her beautiful when she'd been a young girl under fifteen and Connor was twenty-five, hanging in crowds with teenagers. The popular kids in the neighborhood had pushed him around a lot, but she didn't think it would come to him killing that young girl all those years ago.

"Where's Leo?" She swallowed a huge lump in her throat.

"I tried to stop," Connor replied, slowly stepping toward her.

"What did you do?"

Connor's jaw grated as he tried to keep his temper from getting out of control. He'd waited this long to have her in his presence, and nothing would stand in his way. Jessica looked from her right to left, stumbling to move around the coffee table. The house was cluttered in books, clothes, and newspapers.

"They weren't obedient," Connor spoke softly.

"Connor."

His eyes bored into hers.

Jessica slid the ashtray into her hand, behind her back, and gripped it tight.

"Where is Leo?"

"I just wanted to have fun like I used to do."

"What do you mean?"

He chuckled, cocked his head back, and breathed in the air.

"At the barn, held them by their throat as they tried to escape."

"You killed her."

"Alison was special. She talked about you."

"What did she say?"

"Enough talking." Connor charged at Jessica, right as she gripped the ashtray and knocked Connor on the side of the head. He stumbled back in pain, sliding down the wall. Jessica dropped the ashtray and ran to the back hallway.

"Leo!"

She went to the side door, pushed it open to the bathroom, and saw it was empty. Looking back over her shoulder, she saw that Connor was still down on the floor. She went to the kitchen and saw it was empty, glanced around, and picked up the knife off the table. In the corner, she noticed a door, ran over, gripped the knob, and yanked it open. Not waiting for any backup, she went down the stairs, held the knife in her hands, and saw the entire basement was decorated with pictures of dead bodies.

"Oh, my God." Jessica heard groaning and looked to her right, where she saw Leo on the ground. She ran toward him and helped him to sit up.

"Leo, get up, come on. We have to get out of here," Jessica whispered, scanning the basement again.

"Jessica," Leo mumbled, opened his eyes, and leaned up on his knees.

"Yeah, we need to get out of here and call backup."

"What happened?"

"Connor is the one that killed Alison."

"Shit, my head." Leo stood, and Jessica held him up by putting his arm around her neck.

"Come on, we have to hurry up." Jessica helped him climb the stairs one by one.

"We need to call for backup," Leo said, feeling the back of his head.

"Once we get out of here."

They nudged the door open and walked in the kitchen and turned toward the living room. Jessica saw that Connor wasn't there any longer.

"He's gone."

"Stay behind me." Leo pushed her behind him, removed his gun, and patted his pockets for his cellphone.

"Damn it, he took my phone."

"I forgot mine in the car."

Jessica glanced around the kitchen for a phone but didn't see anything.

"Stay behind me." Leo gripped the gun tight, his eyes scanning the surroundings left to right, his breathing controlled and heart pounding. Sweat dripped down his cheeks, and as soon as he stepped a foot out of the kitchen, Connor leaped in front of him, reaching a hand out to take the gun out his hands. Leo held on, punching him in the side of his stomach, and they fell against the wall together.

"Leo!" Jessica shouted, dodging the gun that was waving in the air.

"Arghhh!" Connor screamed as Leo Headbutt him and punched him in the gut. Leo grasped the gun as Connor's eyes narrowed into slits. Connor gritted his teeth, looked to the desk beside him grabbed the lamp, and hit Leo over the head. He dropped the gun on the floor as he went down.

"Leo!" Jessica bent down and grabbed the gun before Connor could retrieve it.

"Give me the gun, Jessica." Connor wiped the blood off his chin.

"Don't move." Jessica kept her eyes on Connor nervously. Leo was the professional; he was used to killing people and not giving it another thought. For Jessica, being a journalist was her thing, but in order to get out of this predicament, she had to save her own life and Leo's. That day when she heard Alison's voice, something within her died, and the thought of Connor being the last person with her broke Jessica's heart.

"What are you going to do, Jessica? Huh...you're just a little girl." Connor taunted her, leaned forward, chuckled, and sat back up.

"That's your thing."

"What?" His mouth flattened into a thin frown.

"We both know you don't have what it takes to get a girlfriend. So you forced yourself on them." Jessica slowly stepped over to Leo. If she could check his pulse, then get to the car and grab her phone, maybe they could get help.

"They were sluts, taunting me, like I didn't mean a thing."

"They were children!" Jessica screamed, reached down, and placed her index and middle finger against Leo's neck.

"Stop it! Alison remembered me so I had to get rid of her."

"You won't get away with this."

"As people, we all have different sides to ourselves. Alison showed me hers. We bonded."

"Shut up!"

"You should have seen her eyes when she recognized me from the barn."

"Don't move."

"I'm going to do the same to you." Connor pulled a knife from behind his back and thrust it toward Jessica. Before she could warn him to stop, the gun went off in her hands.

Pop! Pop! Pop!

"Arghhh!" Connor dropped the knife, fell to his knees and landed face down, with blood pouring from his chest, arm, and leg.

"I killed him," Jessica muttered, looking down at her hands gripped around the gun.

"Jessica..." Leo groggily sat up and took the gun out of her hands.

"Leo... Oh my God!" She wrapped her arms around his neck.

He patted her back soothingly.

"Shushhh...you did what you had to do."

She whimpered in his arms. "I killed him."

Leo stepped out of her hold, kneeled down, and checked his pulse.

"Go grab your phone and call the police."

Jessica nodded, turned, and noticed a picture on the wall of the barn with a group of kids together laughing. Connor was standing in the background with his eyes drawn to the young woman that had been killed that day.

13

Two days later

Jessica Smith took pride in knowing that her work to solve this case wouldn't go in vain and wanted to keep Alison's memory alive. She ran her palm across the bracelet as she stepped into the barn. To see the place rebuilt and standing tall compared to when she was a small child, it didn't look so scary anymore. The town planned on making it a tourist attraction, and she didn't know how to feel about that, but she came down anyway to see her grandparents' house before she flew back to New York. Some teens were outside playing around, and she smiled at the innocence they possessed, their hope for the future.

"Who are you?" A young girl ran out from the barn. She looked no older than twelve or thirteen.

"I'm Jessica. What's your name?"

"Kate."

"Nice to meet you, Kate."

"What are you doing here?"

"Looking around. I used to come here when I was your

age."

"Really?" Her eyes lit up in excitement.

"Yep, me and my three best friends."

"Wow! My friends and I come here too, actually hiding out from them."

"Why?"

"A game we like to play."

"Do your parents know you're here?"

Kate giggled and shook her head. "They told me to stay away, but I don't think it's fair."

"You should listen to your parents."

"They said a girl died here a long time ago, but I think it's a rumor to keep us away."

Jessica froze in place, not knowing if she should continue the conversation.

"Always obey your parents."

"Did you listen to your parents?"

Jessica heard two girls outside yelling Kate's name. "Sometimes."

Kate looked out of the window.

"That's Cameron and Sarah."

"Just be careful and listen to your parents, Kate."

"Okay."

"Kate! Kate!" Sarah and Cameron ran inside the barn, calling her name.

"You didn't give me enough time to hide."

"Your mom is here, and she's mad," Sarah said, pointing outside to the gray Honda parked at the entrance. An older woman in her late forties blocked the sun out with her hand, scanning the area looking for something.

"Probably needs me to babysit," Kate grumbled, heading out of the barn with Sarah and Cameron behind her.

"She said it's getting late." Cameron shrugged her shoulders.

"Kate, remember what I said," Jessica called out.

"I will. Nice meeting you, Jessica." Kate waved, and Cameron nudged her in the shoulder.

"Who's that?"

"Her name is Jessica, and she can hear you." Kate rolled her eyes.

Jessica smiled and released a long-held breath.

"I'll never forget you, Alison."

The ringing startled her out of her thoughts.

"Hello?"

"Jessica, it's Leo."

"What's up, Leo?"

"We need to talk."

"Uhm, I'm not in New York."

"Where are you?"

"My grandparents still live in Tennessee."

"When are you back in the city?"

"Late tomorrow night."

"You owe me dinner. Remember the charity gala coming up."

"I hate dressing up, Leo."

"You promised."

"Let me think it over."

"I can give you two days."

"What's the catch?"

"It's a charity event with a lot of bigwigs."

"Sounds tempting.

"You're a journalist, Jessica. Anything is tempting if you can spin it into a story."

~

I HOPE you enjoyed Jessica's story so far. Please also check out "**Mirror of Lust (A Jessica Smith Mystery) Book 2**" here **www.authoravasking.com** with a host of characters intertwined. Also, if you love Thriller, Mystery, and Suspense, check out **Agent Red: Fatal Memory Book 1 here** https://books2read.com/u/4j2PYX . Another Thriller, Crime Fiction "**Christina Harris**" short here **www.authoravasking.com**.

Download a free short here *"The Firm"* https://payhip.com/b/py7S

Grab Boxset "**Agent Red 1-3**" here https://payhip.com/b/1KcxY

Catch up with "**Agent Red:Fatal Enemy Book 5**" here "https://books2read.com/u/bQJWVE

THE FIRM A SHORT SHORT BONUS EXCERPT

Chapter 1

Flashback Iraq Gulf War.

They'd been working securing the local market earlier in the day and making sure nothing was out of the ordinary. As the last of the team to be in Iraq after the gulf war to clean up, Officer Abraham, Officer Simpson packed up any leftover documents or intel. They both returned to the bunker and informed their General William Jones of a few documents they'd found in a trash can at a street market. Officer Abraham was asked to stay and explain exactly what he saw earlier.

"What do you think this is?" General Jones asked.

"I'm not sure, sir. We did a sweep of the area and saw this in the trash next to the market."

General Jones lifted the documents and scanned them, noticing a few familiar names.

"Can Simpson be trusted?" General questioned.

"Yes, Sir."

"I've heard he's been complaining to anyone that listens. I need him under control." General Jones demanded.

"Yes, Sir."

"That means by any means, Officer Abrahams. About differently. He's been talking a lot of wants to go back home."

Officer Abraham shifted his stance and looked uncomfortable at Officer Simpson's suggestion of not supporting this mission. They've had long talks about their families and what they want to do when returning home on US soil.

"Keep an eye on him." General Jones stated.

"Yes, Sir." Officer Abrahams lifted his hand and saluted Officer Jones as he turned and left out office after being dismissed. General Jones sat back in his seat and looked over the documents and saw Senator names, elected officials from other countries. Something like this to be out in the open was strange to him, and he needed to find out what it meant. He lifted the phone and dialed a number of an old colleague that works in the CIA.

"This better be good," Stanton spoke groggily.

"I wouldn't call unless it was important."

Stanton looked over at his wife in bed and turned to rise out of bed, grab his robe, and head to his office.

"What's going on?"

"One of my soldiers found a list of documents with numbers. I'm not sure if it means anything, but I want to make sure."

"Where did they find it?"

"A trash can at the local market in town."

Stanton sat down in his chair and rubbed his forehead and turned on his computer. He heard rustling on the other end of the phone.

"Maybe it's trash," Stanton replied.

"I would normally agree, but a few names popped up."

"What do you mean?"

"Senators and politicians are on the list."

"Can they be trusted not to talk? Did they read the documents?" Stanton inquired.

"I explained the seriousness of what they brought back.

"Good, send me what you've found, and I'll make some calls," Stanton stated.

"If this comes up to be nothing, then I'll just owe you a beer." General Jones said.

"I agree, but if something more is here, I'll keep you updated."

General Jones hung the phone up and stared at the documents one more time before scanning them in his computer and sending them off to Stanton. Officer Jones didn't know that back in Brooklyn, New York, a local young gamer Mason Stuart was up at three am on his computer hacking government agency computers and finding anything to sell to foreign agencies to make money.

...

Same Day.

The light drops of rain poured down on the window outside of the Whitehouse. It was late in the early mornings, and Vice President Turner informed President Chambers of an emergency in Brooklyn, New York. For the past few weeks, The President, Vice President, and the Director of National Security held meetings earlier about starting an agency beyond the normal security steps outside of the CIA, FBI, and Secret Service. President Chambers was in his third year and was transparent, and now the Vice President and Director built a radical team to protect US interests. Chambers walked into the situation room. The President held a hard grimace on his face.

"Mr.President, we have a situation." Kane Hall, Director of National Security, said.

"What's the problem that you woke me up this late?" President checked his watch and rubbed a hand down his face.

"Stanton received a phone call from General Jones about something he found in Iraq."

"So what's the big deal?" President Chamber said.

The Director and Vice President glanced at each other before looking back at the President.

"Your names on the list, Sir," Kane spoke.

"Who else is on it?" President chambers asked.

"Senators and Congressmen from other foreign countries."

"Are you thinking this is a terrorist attack?" The President asked.

"Possibly, but we need to continue investigating. Another issue has come up." Kane says and passed the President a file on Mason Stuart.

"Who is this?"

"A local gamer in Brooklyn hacked into General Jones's computer and found the list," Kane said.

President Chambers looked up at Kane and Vice President Turner with a right brow lifted.

"How did he get into the system? I thought this was unable to be breached." Chambers said.

"We have someone looking into Mason now, Sir," Kane explained.

"If this gets around before we can investigate, this could be bad." Chambers said.

"We have a solution to buy us some time, Sir," Kane replied.

"Which is?"

"Bring him here and erase any trace of this before we can figure everything out," Turner informed.

"That's fine, and I need the Governors and Presidents informed."

"We think that is a bad idea, sir," Jane said.

"What do you mean?"

"If this is bigger than we think, that would only cause people to hide even deeper. We need to bring them out, and keeping this under wraps between us is the best. Along with a few people to handle the mission." Kane said, lifted the computer screen's remote, and tapped to show five soldiers' photos on the screen.

"What's this?" Chambers said.

"We talked about bringing on a small team to control certain situations that keep the hands of the whitehouse clear. These are the people we feel would work best." Kane said. A photo of Stanton, Henson, Abraham, Beckett, and Davis.

"The Firm and elite squad to handle what we can't deal with on our own without bringing attention to the Whitehouse and our establishment," Turner said.

" Can they be trusted?" Chambers asked.

"Yes, Mr. President," Kane responded.

"What loose ends do we need to take care of?"

"We have already handled them, sir," Kane said.

...

A gunshot went off, and Officer Abraham stared at his fellow soldier, Officer Simpson's dead body, as he laid in the bed sleeping. The next day the local news reported a soldier committing suicide, not knowing Officer Abraham cleaned up any loose evidence to make it seem like a suicide. The local news reports stated a young man named Mason Stuart went missing, and his parents were looking for him. They went on local news stations to get support in finding him alive, but he vanished without a trace. Leaving everything he owned behind in his apartment.A few weeks later, the President established The Firm, a section of elite soldiers to handle top-secret issues from foreign to Domestic.

This is a teaser excerpt of The Firm's beginnings before Teagan Stone was recruited if you want to see more, comment on my blog or email and let me know.

READING ORDER OF SERIES

1.Agent Red-Fatal Memory Book 1
   https://books2read.com/u/4j2PYX
   2.Agent Red-Fatal Target Book 2
   https://books2read.com/u/bWP8Jq
   3.Agent Red-Fatal Crime Book 3
   https://books2read.com/u/mZadZJ
   4.Agent Red-Fatal Justice Book 4
   https://books2read.com/u/mqo7wd
   5. Agent Red-Fatal Enemy Book 5
   https://books2read.com/u/bQJWVE

WHAT'S NEXT?

Want to know what happens next? Follow me at the links below to catch the next release.

Thank you so much for reading, and if you enjoyed the crazy ride and decided to leave a review, we'd truly appreciate the support. Reviews are the lifeblood of the publishing world. They're read, appreciated, and needed. Please consider taking the time to leave a few words on Goodreads or BookBub.

Sign up for updates and sneak peeks at the sites below:

ACKNOWLEDGMENTS

I want to thank my team, who helps me behind the scenes, from my editors to my test readers and graphic designers, and the list goes on. I appreciate each of you for keeping me on my toes.

ABOUT THE AUTHOR

Ava S. King is the debut author of thriller, mystery, suspense, and psychological crime novels.

If you want to know when the next book will come out, please visit my website at http://www.authoravasking.com, where you can sign up to receive an email for her next release.